Oregon Trail 1848

UNORGANIZED TERRITORY

INDEPENDENCE ROCK

CHIMNEY ROCK

IOWA

FORT LARAMIE

INDEPENDENCE

MISSOURI

JOSH FULTON

WILLIE FULTON

SUSAN FULTON

MARY HASTINGS

TEXAS

ARKANSAS

VOICES
from the
OREGON
TRAIL

by KAY WINTERS · *illustrated by* LARRY DAY

DIAL BOOKS *for* YOUNG READERS *An imprint of Penguin Group (USA) LLC*

CARL HAWKS

···◆···

WE LEAVE TODAY, APRIL 25, 1848.
    Two thousand miles to the Promised Land.
We're in Independence, Missouri,
the jumping off place for the Oregon Trail.
I'm Carl Hawks,
son of the captain of this wagon train.
Pa says I'm his right hand,
though I just turned thirteen.
I deliver messages, keep an eye on settlers,
wagons, or livestock who need help.
Pass the word to my pa.

There are thirty-five wagons starting out
from Court House Square.
I've taken the trail twice before.
But who knows what lies ahead?

This time I hope we'll cross rivers
without any drownings,
pass through Indian lands without trouble,
make it to Oregon before the snow flies.

Will anyone catch cholera or measles?
Will we bury many along the trail?
Who will have a baby or get married?

How many of us will survive?

WHAT WILL HAPPEN THIS TIME?

PATIENCE MILLS

—◇—

THIS MORNING WE LEFT INDEPENDENCE FOR OREGON.
I'm a farmer's wife,
wed to Horace, mother of Rachel and Missy.
It was February when Horace told me we were going.
He marched into the kitchen and said,

> *Patience, I sold the farm.*
> *Our neighbors are going West.*
> *I won't be left behind.*
> *There are 640 free acres to be had.*
> *So many trees you can't see the sky.*
> *We're going to Oregon!*

Missy, the three-year-old, was sleeping.
I bade Rachel keep watch,
slipped out to the little grave
behind the house, and wept.

I stooped over Steven's stone.
He died when he was born.
I pulled a thistle.
How could I leave him behind?
But I did
and we're on our way.

HORACE SOLD THE FARM.

ZEBULON FULTON

SPRING TOOK HER SWEET TIME COMING.
We couldn't leave Iowa till the grass greened up
and the cattle could feed.
But at last, we're on our way.
I'm a carpenter by trade,
and Oregon is tall with trees.

For months we've been getting ready.
Me and my boys, Willie and Josh,
built the wagon beds.
We bent hickory bows to hold canvas tops,
greased wheels with tallow to help them turn.
Ma and the girls spun, wove, and stitched shirts, pants,
and dresses before we left.
Ma brought her good dishes,
packed them fancy plates in a barrel of cornmeal.

The Sunday clothes, the family Bible,
the parlor mirror wrapped in quilts,
and some flower seeds
are stored in the wooden trunk.
My carpenter tools are safe in a box.
My rifle's loaded. I'm ready to fight them redskins.

Each of our wagons holds 2,000 pounds.
And we're going more than 2,000 miles.
In Independence we bought bacon, lard, sugar, and flour.
We met Captain Hawks and his son, Carl.
Carl and the captain like to hunt.
And so do we!
　　　Rabbits and turkeys take cover! bragged Josh.
　　　And maybe a buffalo! said Willie.

LOUISA BAILEY

A BUGLE BLARES.
Our Cave Springs campground comes to life.
I'm Louisa, just turned fourteen.
Old enough to get married!
My sisters and I start our chores.

Mama says,
Milk the cows. Pour the milk into the churn.
      Then hang it on the back. Let it bump till suppertime,
          so we'll have butter with our biscuits.

Lucy, Sally, and I do Mama's bidding.
By breakfast the men have rounded up
horses, cattle, and yoked the oxen.
We eat piles of pancakes, beans with bacon,
wash it down with coffee.
      It's like a picnic! Lucy says.
The bugle sounds.
We scoop the cookware up, and damp the fire.
      Roll the wagons! Captain Hawks shouts.
His son, Carl, leads the way.

Papa snaps the whip. GEE HAW! We're off.
Today we're the end of the train.
Our wagons sail forward.
White canvas covers fill with breeze like ships at sea.
The captain says tomorrow we'll be first.
Then thirty-four days till we are last again.

CAPTAIN HAWKS

IT AIN'T EASY TO BE CAPTAIN.
All these emigrants look to me to stay alive.

After my wife died, I left Missouri,
trekked west to keep from sorrowing.
Carl was old enough to come along.
My brother, Nate, joined us last year,
drives the supply wagon, cooks our meals.
He's a blacksmith and a fiddler,
skills that serve us well.

Overlanders are harder to herd than cattle.
They like to rule, but not be ruled.
Each man thinks he's right, wants to be the boss.

Oh, we form a council.
Men have their say.
But in the end I am the one who decides.
>   We go or stay till the storm stops,
>   the river goes down, the grave is dug,
>   the babe is born.
And all the while the days march on,
winter waiting in the wings.

Yup, I'm captain.
And I'm proud to lead the train.
I know the trail,
but I can't outguess the weather,
the current, the quicksand, the cholera,
or know if the Indians are still friendly.

We're coming up on a river crossing.
Storm clouds off to the west.
We have to hustle!

MARY HASTINGS

I'M JUST A FARM GIRL, FEARED OF WATER.
I can churn butter, plant, sew, feed livestock, but I can't swim.
The captain's son rides by and shouts . . . *council meeting.*
My husband, Amos, brings back the news.

>*The river's up from last week's rain.*
>*We need to cross now before the storm.*
>*Mary, hold Caleb tight.*

Easy to say. Hard to do.
Caleb's only three, but he's a kicker!
Some of the men herd the livestock over.
At last we start across.
I keep the whip in one hand,
grasp Caleb with the other.

Amos guides the oxen in the water.
Buck stumbles, turns the wrong way.
The others follow.
Amos grabs Buck's head and turns him back.
I snap the whip. The wagon tilts. Will it tip?

Caleb squirms. I clutch him tight. He howls.
The oxen swim, the wagon rights and floats.
Water rushes over our laps.
We inch toward the other side. I breathe again.

The wagon jerks, a sickening lurch.
Caleb slips over the side.

>I stand and scream . . .
>
>*Caleb . . . Caleb . . . Where's my boy!*
>
>Captain Hawks, Nate, and Amos go after him.

But Caleb's gone . . . vanished . . . disappeared.

Swallowed by dark water.

Josh Fulton

◆

WE MADE THE PLATTE RIVER VALLEY BEFORE DARK.
Pa says,
> *I hear the army is going to build a new fort near here.*
> *Their troops will come to protect Overlanders from Indians.*

Protect us???? I just want to see some.

> *I hear Indians attack wagon trains,* I say.
> *They scalp settlers.*

The twins scream and shriek. GIRLS!
Ma shudders and mutters,
> *I wish I'd never come.*
> *River crossings . . . drownings . . . Indians . . . graves.*

Pa gives me a swat and says,
> *See what you started! Shut your mouth!*

My older brother, Willie, snickers.

I keep quiet, but I think it's true.
I'm only twelve, but even I know Indians have tomahawks.
Everybody knows Indians are savages.
I've heard Pa say so himself!

Ma changes the subject.
> *Carl told me we could leave letters*
> *at Ash Hollow for turn-arounds to carry back.*

She's been scribbling to her sisters and Grandma.
They were sorrowful to see us go.

After supper, once the campfire fades,
Mr. Bailey, Pa, Willie, and I keep watch.
As we look up, Mr. Bailey says,
> *Never seen so many stars.*
> *Sky and land seem to stretch forever . . .*
> *Makes me feel like a tiny speck!*

I don't mention Indians!

RACHEL MILLS

I'M RACHEL. JUST ELEVEN, SAME AS LUCY BAILEY.
Today we pick bluebells and buttercups,
weave wreaths for each other, and the oxen.
Carl rides by, lets out a whoop and points.

That's Chimney Rock up ahead, he says.
It'll take two days to get there.
Wait till you see all the names carved
by folks who've come this way.

We've seen sadder signs of those who've gone before, I say.
Yesterday I counted twelve graves dug up by wolves.

There ARE some scary times, says Lucy.
But I'm still glad we're going,
*   and I think my sister Louisa's sparking with Willie.*
Watch how they sit together tonight at campfire.
We giggle.
*   It's like a traveling town, I say.*

Two days later we noon at Chimney Rock.
Suddenly the sky darkens, wind rises.
Hail the size of snowballs pelts our heads.
We bolt for our wagons.

The left corner of our canvas r—i—p—s.
The horses rear and whinny.
Carl, Willie, and Josh run by,
pots on their heads to dodge the hail.
The boys tie the animals fast.
As quickly as the storm starts, it stops.
Mother and I take out our needles
and slowly stitch us up.

CHANKOOWASHTAY

···— · · ◇ · · —···

HERE THEY COME.
More and more wagons on wheels,
like clouds that stretch across the sky.
Where will it end?

I'm Chankoowashtay, a Sioux scout.
These strangers fish our streams ... drink our water ... kill the buffalo,
leave what they do not want rotting in the dust.

I try to tell the chief ...
but he has not been warned in the dreaming time.
He just nods, looks at his fire, and keeps his council.

The wagons slow their wheels
near Fort Laramie. Stop for the night.
Our women offer moccasins for trade.
The braves eye the horses.
Our old ones look at livestock.
Their women sit like stones.
They sniff the air and wrinkle their noses
as if they smell something bad.

Where will this end?
Wave after wave of wagons on wheels.
What will happen to my people,
        to the land,
                to the game?

NO GOOD CAN COME OF THIS.

ABIGAIL BAILEY

I'T'S THE FOURTH OF JULY!
Captain Hawks said if we made Independence Rock by today
we *might* get to Oregon before the snow flies.

I'm Abigail. Wed to Benjamin,
mother of Lucy, Louisa, and Sally,
and about to give birth again.

Two other folks have died besides Caleb.
The Miller boys were swallowed in quicksand
when we crossed the River Platte.
Makes me fearful for my little one to come.

After supper my daughter Lucy and her friend Rachel
follow Nate and his fiddle up the rock.
A parade of pioneers.
Benjamin, Sally, and I climb more slowly.

Willie Fulton twirls Louisa around,
her red calico a-swirl.
He writes Louisa's name in buffalo grease
on the southeast point of the rock.

I told you they were sparking! I say to Benjamin.
There'll be a wedding afore this trip is done, he says.
Be glad to have a son in Oregon.
Willie's a worker. His dad's a carpenter.
We'll start a sawmill since there are trees to spare.

Gunshots echo up and down the trail.
Overlanders celebrating Independence Day.

HORACE MILLS

ME? I'M A FARMER. BUT NOT A STAY-AT-HOME.
I love moving on.
We're rolling alongside the Sweetwater.
Carl says we're in Cheyenne country.
Suddenly the ground begins to rumble.
I look for braves on horseback,
but the plains are black with buffalo.
Hooves thunder, pound the ground.
Coming close . . . closer. . . .
We men and several women take out rifles.

Suddenly the herd turns,
heads for the wagons.
The women scream. The girls shriek.
Shoot, Captain Hawks shouts, firing in the air.
Gunshots sound all around.
The herd turns and runs to the right of us.
A tale to tell!

Carl, Nate, Captain Hawks, Zebulon, the Fulton boys, Ben Bailey,
and I follow the buffalo trail.
We bring down two black bulls.

Captain Hawks shows us how to take the tongue,
meat from the hump, and marrow bones.
> *We'll leave the rest for wolves,* he says.
> Carl says, *If we were Indians, we'd take it all.*

Mrs. Mills invites the captain, Nate, and Carl to come for supper.
We feast on buffalo,
a treat after days of bacon and beans.
That night, as our wagons circle,
we watch stars shoot
across the prairie sky.

Lucy Bailey

BUFFALO CHIPS! HORRID STINKY BUFFALO CHIPS!
Plop! Josh Fulton fling chips at Sally and me.
Plop! Sally and I pelt him back.
We fire chips to and fro, dodging and darting.
  Lucy Bailey! thunders Pa.
  Stop that! Those chips feed our fire. Our fire feeds us.
I hang my head. Josh disappears.
Here come Rachel and Missy;
Missy and Sally point at the prairie dogs
popping in and out of holes, playing hide-and-seek.
Wish we could have one for a pet.

I see a grave with a tiny sunbonnet
tied to wooden cross. The day dims.
  Rachel, I say, *Mama's going to have a baby.*
  I overheard her talking to Pa.
  We've made it through South Pass.
  But we're only halfway to Oregon.
Rachel frowns, but she says,
  Lucy, we've come a thousand miles.
  Your mama's strong.

  She IS a good birther, I say,
  but having a baby out here makes me fearful.

Rachel grabs my hand.
  Captain Hawks will call a halt when her time comes.
  Mrs. Fulton's a midwife. Your sister Louisa will help.

Rachel speaks brighter than I feel.
Usually I'm the one who cheers her.
But today my spirit flags, my courage falters.
  I keep seeing that sunbonnet.

NATE HAWKS

I WIPE SWEAT OFF MY FACE.
August already.
Folks don't know it, and I won't tell them,
but the worst of the trip is still ahead.

The Overlanders are wore out.
Weary from walking, worried about surviving.
Last night there was a fistfight over standing watch.
The captain tries to settle squabbles with a light hand.
I play my fiddle to set toes tapping, help keep the peace.

The oxen are dragging.
Some wagons bought in Independence have wobbly wheels.
When we camp I weld new rims to set the tires.

We've still got the Snake River
and the Cascade Mountains to cross.
Zebulon Fulton is weak with mountain fever.
This morning six more oxen were found dead.

At the Council Meeting comes unwelcome news.
    The oxen are too weak now to pull heavy loads.
    Once again we have to leave more goods behind.

Folks grumble, but they put out cookstoves,
 tables, chests, and books.
Mrs. Fulton leaves her barrel of good dishes.
    Too fancy for where we're going, she said,
but I heard her sigh.
The rocker of Mrs. Mills sways slowly in the breeze.

At Fort Hall we trade lame cattle for pounds of flour.
And on we go.

Susan Fulton

— ⋯ ◆ ⋯ —

I am Zebulon's wife.
I mother of Josh, Willie, and the twins.
I'm also a midwife. Abigail Bailey is almost due.
She's counting on me to help with the birthing.

We are DRENCHED IN DUST.
We breathe dust, feel dust, eat dust. I hate dust!
It coats our wagons, our beds, ourselves.

The dreaded Snake River is up ahead.
Maybe there we can have a wash.
  The Snake has a powerful current, Captain Hawks warns.
I can't forget Caleb in that dark water.

Captain Hawks hires some Nez Percé Indians to guide us across.
  They helped Lewis and Clark on their expedition, the captain says.
The Nez Percé swim and hold the oxen by their yokes.

Suddenly Carl Hawks's horse rears and tosses him into the stream.
He's caught in the current. He disappears.
  No! Not another drowning. Where IS he?
I strain to see.
The water rushes wildly by.
    Over there! Josh points.
Carl is bobbing in the current.
He grabs a stump, holds fast with both hands.
The Nez Percé pull him into their canoe
and paddle swiftly to the other side.
    Josh shouts . . . *Let's hear it for the Nez Percé!*

THE NEZ PERCÉ!

BENJAMIN BAILEY

— ◇ —

I'M STANDING GUARD BY OUR WAGON.
I WAAAH . . . . WAAAH . . . .

Did the baby come? Lucy asks.
Your brother, Daniel, I say,
born last night while you and Sally
were sleeping in the tent.

I climb up and give the girls a hand.
Daniel's face is red, his fists are clenched,
his howls are strong.

A new settler for Oregon, said Abigail.
And we didn't even have to lay over!

Louisa cooks our breakfast.

A new baby and now your wedding! I say.

The wait is over, Louisa said. Willie and I are ready.
I have Grandmother's cameo.
Mrs. Mills has a lace tablecloth I can use for a veil.
Lucy, will you and Rachel pick sunflowers?

Two days later
Captain Hawks conducts the ceremony.
I give Louisa away and gain two sons in just one week!
Now we can plan our sawmill.

Nate tunes his violin. Music dances through the campsite.
When the fire dies and the camp is still,
outside their wagon, the shivaree starts.
Pots bang, horns blare, whistles blow, bells ring.
Settlers serenade them . . .
Newlyweds!

WILLIE FULTON

WE'RE TAKING THE BARLOW ROAD.
   The wagons struggle over branches, sink into mud holes,
bump around stumps, fallen trees, and boulders.
Bodies and bones of dead horses, oxen, and cows line the path.
I breathe through my mouth, start the steep climb up Laurel Hill.

When we get to the top,
I gasp . . . *We have to go down this?*
Carl mutters. *It's a three-hundred-foot drop. Straight down!*
     Last time the rope broke,
     a wagon skidded and shattered at the bottom.
     Two people were killed. But don't tell the girls.

Don't tell the girls? I wish he hadn't told me.
We wrap ropes around the redwoods to slow the wheels.

We tie logs to the back of the wagons to act as brakes.
Then slowly, ever so slowly, with a line of other settlers,
we let . . . the . . . ropes . . . out.
     Inch by inch.
     Inch by inch.
Our wagon lurches.
The rope stretches out . . . h-o-l-d-s.
I stand frozen in place.

Down . . . down . . . down the wagons creep to the bottom.
We help one another.
Then I make my way on foot.
Laurel Hill . . . we'll never forget YOU.

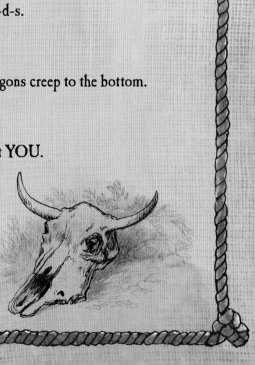

CARL HAWKS

···—·—◆—·—···

OREGON CITY!
Whistling, whooping, cheering, pounding on pots,
we stand on a bluff looking down.
A few houses, stores, a church steeple urge us onward.
Snow sparkles behind us on Mount Hood.
Below a ferry crosses the Willamette River.
We've traveled more than 2,000 miles.

Here come some settlers from last year's trip.
Welcome, one says shaking my hand.
So glad you made it!
How was the trip this time? his wife asks.

Not bad, I say.
Seven wagons turned back. Four folks died.
But no one caught cholera or measles.
No Indians attacked.
The Nez Percé helped us across the Snake.
They saved my hide!
We had a wedding and a birthing.

Laurel Hill? asks the settler with a shudder.

We made it safely down.
My pa brought most of us the whole way, I say with pride.

Some day I'd like to lead a wagon train.
It sure beats farming in Missouri.
I wonder if we'll stay in Oregon.
I'd miss Josh, Lucy, and Rachel if we go,
but we've heard talk of gold in California.

Think of it!
GOLD!

❖ HISTORICAL NOTES ❖

The journey across the Oregon Trail is one of America's great epic stories. In 1836, missionaries Marcus and Narcissus Whitman and Henry and Elizabeth Spaulding traveled to the Oregon Territory with wagons. Although their wagons didn't go the full distance, the Whitmans proved that women and wheels *could* make the journey. Letters to the newspaper and to relatives back home from early travelers, called *overlanders*, described the "promised land." Tantalized by tales of pumpkins so big that one could be hollowed to make a barn, turnips that grew five feet around, trees so tall the timber of one would build a cabin, or fat fresh pigs that ran around already cooked—ready to be eaten—men who were restless, men called *movers on* in those days, burned with *Oregon fever*. Their wives and children came, too, most of whom had no choice. Many were reluctant. One out of every five females was pregnant. Many had small children. Most had to leave relatives and friends behind.

WHEN DID THEY GO?

From the 1830s through the 1860s, thousands of overlanders trekked across the plains. After 1869 when the Central and Union Pacific Railroad began running, the trip west took a week instead of six months. Wagons still went. They were a cheaper alternative, but the numbers were greatly reduced.

WHY DID THEY GO?

Most emigrants left their homes in search of rich free land that could be profitably farmed, unlike the thin overworked soil they currently had. By 1843 free land was promised to the head of each household who settled in Oregon by the provisional government of Oregon. Married couples could claim up to 640 acres at no cost. Many wanted to escape the depression that began in 1837 when banks closed, farms were foreclosed, home mortgages could not be paid. Health was the reason some went. Typhoid, scarlet fever, tuberculosis, and malaria had taken their toll. The Mormons trekked with their handcarts, in search of religious freedom. Patriotism was another reason. By settling Oregon, that part of the country could be claimed by the United States. And *Oregon fever* was not to be denied. Many of the emigrants had moved before. Some several times. Moving meant a fresh start, a new place, an adventure.

By 1849 huge numbers were crowding the trail, but many turned south to head to California in search of gold, a different dream. After July of 1848, two-thirds of the males who traveled to Oregon left for California to pursue that dream.

WHAT KIND OF WAGONS?

The overlanders used farm wagons. Some built their own. Many bought new ones in Independence or Saint Joseph, Missouri. The wagons were narrow, approximately four feet wide and ten feet long. They were made of maple or oak with hoops over which canvas was pulled creating a bonnet. The front wheels were smaller than the back, which helped the wagon turn. The wagons rolled along on wheels with iron tires, and were usually drawn by teams of four oxen, directed by an overlander walking. Some emigrants used mules, but mules were harder to handle.

HOW WERE THE WAGON TRAINS ORGANIZED?

Organization varied with each wagon train. In the early days, mountain men frequently were hired as guides or pilots. Captains were elected, sometimes many times during one trip. A constitution was drawn up. Council meetings were held on a regular basis. Only men could attend. Later, some groups paid an experienced captain or wagon master to be their leader and relied on him to make crucial decisions. Council meetings continued to be held, with input from the overlanders. Scouts rode horseback from the front of the train to the back, keeping an eye on the travelers and calling halt if a wagon broke down, a babe was about to be born, or a child fell out. Scouts also went far afield to check out buffalo, elk, Indians, or possible water supplies. Everyone from four years old up worked. A watch was held every night with rotating guard duty.

Depending on the width of the trail, wagons came one behind the other, or spread out in four or five trains in the hope of avoiding dust. Except for the driver of the wagon, babies, toddlers who couldn't keep up, or someone who was sick, emigrants walked most of the 2,000 miles. The goal was 15–20 miles a day. They couldn't move too quickly or the animals would tire. They couldn't move too slowly or blizzards would trap them later in the mountains.

WHAT SUPPLIES DID THEY TAKE?

They brought food, tools, clothes, cooking gear, sewing supplies, medicine, bedding, keepsakes, and some furniture. Many brought cows to milk and extra oxen. Some brought chickens. As the train progressed, the wagons had to be halted several times while overlanders lightened their loads, leaving treasures behind so they could cross the mountains. One man wept when he had to discard his mother's rolling pin. *Her biscuits were awful good,* he remembered. Large trains often had a supply wagon with extra foodstuffs, chains, ropes, bolts, and tools.

WHERE DID THE TRAIL START?

There were a number of "jumping off" places, but two major ones were Independence and Saint Joseph, Missouri. The towns were fierce rivals, and newspapers and hucksters told lies about the other. Claims of cholera and price gouging were numerous. Businesses in both towns were quick to expand to serve the emigrants. Blacksmiths, wagon salesmen, owners of general stores or stables were eager to share in the profits. Some people came by wagon, others by steamship. Those who came by boat were eager customers for wagons, oxen, and supplies.

WHAT WERE THE HAZARDS?

Accidental shooting of self or others happened regularly. Children fell off wagons and were killed or injured when the wheels rolled over them. Sometimes youngsters wandered off picking berries and were never found. One in five children did not survive. Diseases like mountain fever, dysentery, and measles plagued the travelers. And starting in 1849, cholera ran through wagon trains sometimes wiping out the entire group. Births were challenging. There was little time to stop and wait. River crossings were dreaded. Some had rapids, quicksand, or soft spots which could trap horses or oxen. Occasionally wagons overturned in the water and people drowned. Coming down steep inclines like Laurel Hill was death defying. Diaries offered differing accounts of how the wagons inched their way down.

NATIVE AMERICANS

Hollywood has greatly exaggerated the idea of Native Americans lying in wait to ambush wagon trains. In fact in the early 1840s, most of the encounters that early travelers had with Indians were positive, although some young braves considered it a challenge or game to steal horses. The natives were eager to trade, curious about the wagons, the women, and livestock. They tasted the food of the travelers, and often plucked settlers from raging rivers, ferried their goods in dugout canoes, helped them down steep inclines, or shared their salmon. But after the 1850s when the tribes saw that the trains kept coming, that the buffalo herds were depleted, and trigger happy army personnel massacred whole settlements, Indian attacks became more frequent.

GRAVE SITES

Wagon trains handled the matter of funerals and grave sites in various ways. In the beginning of the trip many trains would halt for a service—sometimes for half a day. But as the wagons traveled on, the urgency of arriving sooner rather than later took over. The person was buried, a brief prayer said, and the train moved on. In some places graves were marked with crosses, headboards, or stones. Other groups deliberately buried the person on the trail itself so the wagons would roll over and over the grave, hardening the ground, making the grave invisible.

WHAT WERE THE PLEASURES?

The trail was tough and exhausting, but there *were* happy times. Many emigrants relished the adventure of new sights, sounds, and places. They enjoyed the companionship of one another after living on lonely farms. They relished the music, the scenery, dancing, celebrations like weddings, or the Fourth of July, storytelling around the campfire, and arriving at forts or trading posts. They were delighted with fresh meat from buffalo or antelope. Once they arrived in Oregon, many made plans to live near their new friends.

ARRIVAL IN OREGON CITY

After straggling into Oregon City weary but full of hope, the settlers began their new life. Now they had to build houses, plant crops, or start their new business. But they had arrived! They had endured blistering heat, thirst, hunger, homesickness, rattlesnakes, dysentery, fear, illness, choking dust, death among families, friends, and neighbors. *They had seen the elephant!** They had survived!

They had made new friends, and seen strange sights and new places. They had had adventures with wildlife, weather, and Indians that they never would have experienced on the farm at home. They had a new life, a fresh start, rich soil, and plenty of timber. Three hundred thousand travelers started on the Oregon Trail. Ninety percent arrived at their destination. These pioneers opened up the West.

At last, America stretched from sea to shining sea.

*experienced the worst

✦ NOTE FROM THE AUTHOR ✦

My husband, Earl, and I traveled the Oregon Trail by car for eighteen days in 2008. We stood in wagon ruts, remaining from wagon trains in Nebraska, Wyoming, and Idaho. We explored forts, museums, parks, interpretive trail centers, trading posts, and landmarks. We took pictures, read diaries, heard presentations, asked questions of the interpreters, saw dioramas, films, artifacts, and charts. We tried on pioneer clothing, climbed into wagons, sat around a campfire, heard stories and songs. After climbing Independence Rock we saw names of the emigrants carved in the stone. We attended the Snake River Crossing Re-enactment at Three Island Crossing in Glenns Ferry, Idaho, where we saw how the treacherous current made river crossings a terror for travelers. We groped our way up Laurel Hill in Oregon, marveling that any wagon could make it down that nearly perpendicular slope without crashing. At the Tamástslikt Cultural Center, near Pendleton, Oregon, we went to the Native American–owned interpretive center and learned how the westward expansion changed Indian lives.

✦ FURTHER READING ✦

Armitage, Susan, and Elizabeth Jameson, editors. *The Women's West*. Norman, OK : University of Oklahoma Press, 1987.

*Blackwood, Gary. *Life on the Oregon Trail*. San Diego, CA: Lucent Books, 1999.

Bullard, William C. *Bound for the Promised Land*. City of Independence, MO: National Frontier Trails Center, 1990.

Butruille, Susan G. *Women's Voices from the Oregon Trail*. Boise, ID: Tamarack Books, 1994.

Collings, Kit. *The Oregon Trail. Pioneers Trails West*. Editor, Don Worcester, Caldwell, ID: Caxton Printers, 1985,

*Duncan, Dayton. *The West: An Illustrated History for Children*. Boston: Little Brown, and Company, 1996.

*Fisher, Leonard Everett. *The Oregon Trail*. New York: Holiday House, 1990.

Franzwa, Gregory M. *The Oregon Trail Revisited*. Gerald, MO: Patrice Press, 1982.

*Freedman, Russell, *Buffalo Hunt*. New York: Scholastic, 1988.

_____ *Children of the Wild West*. New York: Clarion Books, 1983.

*Gregory, Kristiana. *Across the Wide and Lonesome Prairie*. New York: Scholastic, 1997.

*Hermes, Patricia. *Westward to Home*. New York: Scholastic, 2001.

Hewitt, James, editor. *Wagon Trains West. Eye-Witnesses to History*. New York: Charles Scribner's Sons, 1973.

Holmes, Kenneth, editor. *Covered Wagon Women: Diaries and Letters from the Western Trails, 1840–1890, Vol. 1-IX*, Glendale, CA: Arthur H. Clark 1983–1990.

*Kimball, Violet. *Stories of Young Pioneers in Their Own Words*. Missoula, MT: Mountain Press, 2000.

*Levine, Ellen. *If You Traveled West in a Covered Wagon*. New York: Scholastic,1986.

_____ *The Journal of Jedediah Barstow, An Emigrant on the Oregon Trail*. New York: Scholastic, 2002.

*Littlefield, Holly. *Children of the Trail West*. Minneapolis, MN: Carolrhoda Books, 1999.

Lockley, Fred. *Voices of the Oregon Territory*. Eugene, OR: Rainy Day Press, 1981.

Luchetti, Cathy. *Children of the West*. New York: W.W. Norton and Co., 2001.

Mattes, Merrill. *The Great Platte River Road*. Nebraska State Historical Society, 1969. Vol. XXV.

Place, Marian T. *Westward on the Oregon Trail*. New York: American Heritage Publishing Company,1962.

Palmer, Joel. *Journals of Travels Over the Oregon Trail in 1845*. Portland, OR: Oregon Historical Society, 1993.

Schlissel, Lillian. *Women's Diaries of the Westward Journey*. Schocken, reprint edition, 2004

*Woodruff, Elvira. *Dear Levi, Letters from the Overland Trail*. New York: A. Knopf, 1994

* Books students might especially enjoy.

❖ ACKNOWLEDGMENTS ❖

The author particularly would like to acknowledge Earl D. Winters. He planned our trip on the trail, worked out timing, routes, and locations. He created a photographic record of our trip, shared in the research along the way, and put his scientific training to work as we assembled and analyzed the information we collected.

I also would like to thank Megan Burt, Education Coordinator, Historic Oregon City, who reviewed the manuscript, searched for appropriate paintings to illustrate locations, never grew impatient with my many questions, and helped me locate obscure research materials.

I am also grateful to R. W. Edwards, Curator of Education at the National Frontier Trails Center, Independence, Missouri. His correspondence with me helped clarify several issues of confusion, and he provided appropriate data to include in the book.

Earl and I especially appreciated the help of Duane and Gisela Ray who live in Oregon. On our trip on the trail, they guided us to Laurel Hill and sent us photographs of prairie flowers.

For my husband, Earl D. Winters, whose love of history ignited my own —K.W.

For Gerald Merfeld, who opened up the world of illustration for me —L.D.

DIAL BOOKS FOR YOUNG READERS ✶ Published by the Penguin Group
Penguin Group (USA) LLC ✶ 375 Hudson Street, New York, New York 10014

USA ✶ Canada ✶ UK ✶ Ireland ✶ Australia ✶ New Zealand ✶ India ✶ South Africa ✶ China
penguin.com

A PENGUIN RANDOM HOUSE COMPANY

Text copyright © 2014 by Kay Winters ✶ Pictures copyright © 2014 by Larry Day

Library of Congress Cataloging-in-Publication Data ✶ Winters, Kay. ✶ Voices from the Oregon Trail/by Kay Winters; illustrated by Larry Day. ✶ pages cm ✶ Summary: "An account of several families and individuals making the long and often dangerous trek across the United States from Missouri to the West Coast in the 1800s"—Provided by publisher. ✶ Includes bibliographical references. ✶ ISBN 978-0-8037-3775-4 (hardcover) ✶ 1. Oregon National Historic Trail—History—Juvenile literature. 2. Overland journeys to the Pacific—Juvenile literature. 3. Frontier and pioneer life—West (U.S.)—Juvenile literature. 4. Pioneers—Oregon National Historic Trail—History—Juvenile literature. I. Day, Larry, date, illustrator. II. Title. F597.W795 2014 978'.02—dc23 2013000034

Manufactured in China on acid-free paper ✶ 10 9 8 7 6 5 4 3 2 1
Designed by Jason Henry ✶ Text set in Caslon Antique ✶ The artwork for this book was created with pencil, pen and ink with watercolor and gouache on watercolor paper.